Go to the Library!

by Charles M. Schulz

Adapted by May Nakamura · Illustrated by Robert Pope

Ready-to-Read

Simon Spotlight

New York   London   Toronto   Sydney   New Delhi

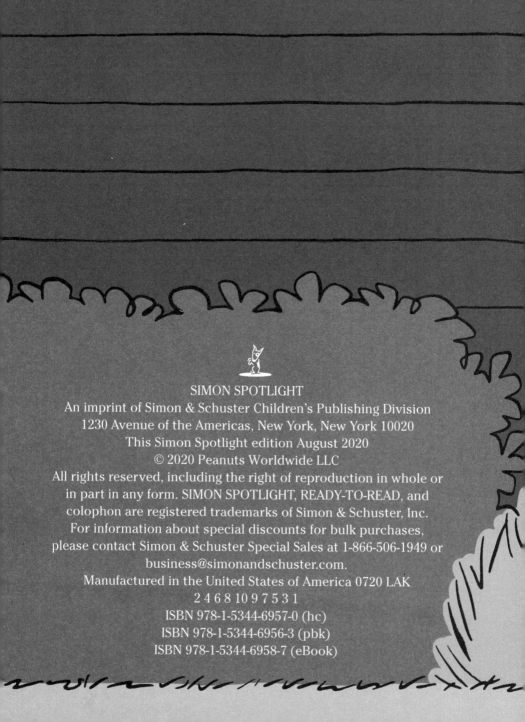

SIMON SPOTLIGHT
An imprint of Simon & Schuster Children's Publishing Division
1230 Avenue of the Americas, New York, New York 10020
This Simon Spotlight edition August 2020
© 2020 Peanuts Worldwide LLC
For information about special discounts for bulk purchases,
please contact Simon & Schuster Special Sales at 1-866-506-1949 or
business@simonandschuster.com.
Manufactured in the United States of America 0720 LAK
2 4 6 8 10 9 7 5 3 1
ISBN 978-1-5344-6957-0 (hc)
ISBN 978-1-5344-6956-3 (pbk)
ISBN 978-1-5344-6958-7 (eBook)

Sally smiled. "Happiness is having your own library card!"

"What is that?"
asked Charlie Brown.

Sally turned to her brother,
who was reading his own book.
"I learned something
very important today,"
she said.

She didn't look up until
the end of the book!

At home Sally settled
into her beanbag
and started reading.

After saying goodbye
to their friends,
Sally and Charlie Brown
left the library.

Sally brought the book
and her library card
to the checkout desk.
The librarian scanned the card
and the book with a machine.
Then she gave Sally a paper slip
printed with the book's due date.

"Really?"
Sally thought about that
for a moment.
Then she declared,
"Libraries are *wonderful*!"

"You don't need any money,"
Linus replied.

"But I don't have any money!"
Sally cried.

Sally found a book
with many pictures inside.
"Now take this book to
the librarian," Charlie Brown said.
"Tell her you'd like to borrow it."

They walked up and down the
aisles.
There were so many books
to choose from!

"Come on, Sally. Let's find
a book for you to check out,"
Charlie Brown said.

"I didn't know dogs were allowed
in the library," she said.
This dog is! Snoopy thought.

A few minutes later Sally spotted
Snoopy and Woodstock
doing a puzzle.

"Good grief,"
Charlie Brown replied.
"I didn't even know
you *had* a book club!"
"Shh! Use your quiet voices
in the library," Linus warned.

Then Lucy walked by.
"I can't believe it!"
she yelled at Charlie Brown.
"You missed
my book club meeting!"

Peppermint Patty wanted to
go outside and play baseball.
"No games until you finish
your book report," Marcie said.

"You can do many things
at the library,"
Charlie Brown said.
He pointed to
Peppermint Patty and Marcie,
who were doing their homework.

Linus, Sally, and Charlie Brown
wandered around the library.
It was full of people.

Ta-da!
She now had her own library card!
"That was easy," she said.

The librarian gave Sally
a plastic card.
Sally carefully wrote her name
on the back, and . . .

She looked up.

"*Know* their librarian?" she said.

"I can't even *see* the librarian!"

Sally took a deep breath
and walked to the librarian's desk.

"This will be a good experience
for you," Charlie Brown replied.
"I think everyone should get to
know their librarian."

Soon they reached the library.
Sally started feeling nervous.
"I've never been inside a library
before," she said.

Sally was so happy
that her Sweet Babboo
was coming along
on her special day!

Sally and her big brother,
Charlie Brown,
walked to the library.
Linus, Sally's Sweet Babboo,
joined them.

It was a special day
for Sally Brown.
She was getting her
very first library card!